12-25-01

Merry Christmas, Michaela

For,

Auntie + Uncle

The Brand New Kid

by
Katie Couric

Illustrated by
Marjorie Priceman

SCHOLASTIC INC.
New York Toronto London Auckland Sydney
Mexico City New Delhi Hong Kong Buenos Aires

To Jay Monahan,

whose love and kindness sustain and guide us every day

Dear Readers,

As a mother watching her two children grow, I am sometimes reminded of difficult lessons from my own childhood . . . that as loving and wonderful as they are, children can sometimes be cruel. Kindness can be taught, and perhaps we can all do a better job helping our children learn about tolerance and inclusion. As a journalist, I have also been struck by the frightening incidents of school violence that can arise from feeling alienated and ostracized. I hope that *The Brand New Kid* can be used as a springboard to talk about the importance of basic human kindness and compassion in our daily lives. Surely, we have all known someone like Lazlo. It sometimes takes courage, but I hope this story will inspire all of us to reach out and make someone feel a little less scared and a little less lonely.

Katie Couric

Ellie McSnelly and Carrie O'Toole
were running and laughing – their first day of school
was today! And they wondered just what was in store.
Would this be a good year? Would school be a bore?

They kept fingers crossed they'd be in the same class,
and on a big table that they had to pass
they checked to find out to which room they should go.
"McSnelly . . . 240, O'Toole, I don't know . . .

Oh, here it is, dear, you're 240 as well."
They squealed with delight, Oh gee, this was swell!
240 meant they would both have Miss Kincaid,
the best teacher by far in the whole second grade.

They took their seats quickly, Miss Kincaid called the roll.
Emily Allen (here!) Tyler Antole . . .
(Here!) Peter Barsinsky, Raquel Brooks (here too!)
She went down the list until she was all through.

Then she got to the boy who was not in her book.
"We have a new student" . . . they all turned to look.
"His name is a different one, Lazlo S. Gasky,
he's new to our school and the town of Delasky.

Please welcome him here, won't you all please say hi?"
But the students just turned and stared at the new guy.
His hair was so blond, why it looked almost white.
It stuck out all over, it didn't look right.
His lips were bright pink, his eyes very blue.
He looked at his feet and he fidgeted too.
He was quiet at first and then yelled out, "Hello."
His voice booming so loud it made Ellie say, "Whoa!"
The other kids laughed, gee this new boy was weird.
Too different and strange to fit in they all feared.

"Now, class," Miss Kincaid said, her voice shrill and tight,
"let's focus on learning and getting things right."
She turned from the students, white chalk was her tool
as she wrote, Welcome Back to Brookhaven School!

They sharpened their pencils and picked up their books,
all morning long, they kept shooting him looks.
They headed to gym class, a quick softball game,
when they went to pick teams, no one mentioned his name.

At lunch, Ricky Jensen, who thought he was cool,
made everyone laugh when he shouted "Hey fool!"

As Lazlo was leaving the line with his tray
someone tripped him, his food it went every which way.
The students all froze as they saw Lazlo's face
with French fries and ketchup all over the place.

So these first weeks were lonely for this brand new kid.
They made fun of him, all that he said and he did.
So he kept his head bowed and stopped trying to please
and simply prepared for the next taunt and tease.

One day after school Ellie walked out the door
and she saw someone she hadn't seen there before.
A lady whose face looked so tired and worn,
she had tears in her eyes and she seemed so forlorn.
"Who is that?" Ellie asked of a student she saw.
"Oh, that's Lazlo's mother," said Susie McGraw.
"Her son's having trouble, she might pull him out,
this school may be wrong for him, she's full of doubt."
Ellie watched Mrs. Gasky as she walked toward her car.
She thought about how things were going so far,
about Lazlo and how he felt different and strange
and wondered aloud just what she could arrange.

"I've got it!" she said. "I'll ask him to play
at my house or his after school ends one day."
The next morning she walked up to him at his locker,
"Would you like to come over and maybe play soccer?"

Stunned, he said, "Please come to my house and play."
So Ellie said, "Sure, I can, let's pick a day."
"How about Thursday?" he asked with a smile,
a look that hadn't been on his face in a while.

They walked home from school with their books in their arms,
passing meadows and fields and a couple of farms.
They arrived at his door greeted by his French poodle
and Mrs. Gasky was there with a plate of warm strudel!

As they munched on the pastry, they made quite a mess
and Lazlo said, "Do you know how to play chess?"
Ellie said, "Yes, but I'm not all that great."
"That's okay," he replied and he soon said "Checkmate!"

The afternoon ended, Ellie said, "This was fun."
Lazlo just smiled and said, "Hey, thanks a ton
for coming to my house and being my friend
at a school in a town where I just don't fit in."

At school the next day the kids stopped her and said,
"You were walking with Lazlo, are you sick in the head?"
Ellie paused and replied, "Now I know him, you see,
Lazlo isn't that different from you and from me.
He's terrific at chess, and his Mom's really sweet.
Playing soccer the guy doesn't have two left feet.
He may look slightly strange, have an accent and stuff,
but if you knew him, you'd like him, it wouldn't be tough."

Carrie looked at her friend and she thought for a while
and when Lazlo walked up she gave him a big smile.

"Hey Ellie! Hey Lazlo! Do you want to go play?"
And they all walked outside on a beautiful day.

ISBN 0-439-28304-3

12 11 10 9 8 7 6 5 4 3 2 1   1 2 3 4 5 6/0

Printed in Mexico   49

First Scholastic printing, September 2001